# The SNOW LION

For Karen and Nina —J. H.

For Phoebe and Kitty —R. J.

Ω

Published by
PEACHTREE PUBLISHERS
1700 Chattahoochee Avenue
Atlanta, Georgia 30318-2112
*www.peachtree-online.com*

Text © 2017 by Jim Helmore
Illustrations © 2017 by Richard Jones

First published in Great Britain in 2017 by Simon and Schuster UK Ltd
1st Floor, 222 Grays Inn Road, London, WC1X 8HB
A CBS Company
First United States version published in 2018 by Peachtree Publishers

The illustrations were rendered in paint and edited in Adobe Photoshop.

Printed in April 2018 by Leo Paper Group in China
10 9 8 7 6 5 4 3 2 1
First Edition

ISBN: 978-1-68263-048-8

Library of Congress Cataloging-in-Publication Data

Names: Helmore, Jim, author. | Jones, Richard, 1977– illustrator.
Title: The snow lion / Jim Helmore and Richard Jones.
Description: Atlanta : Peachtree Publishers, 2018. | Summary: Caro is too shy to make friends in
her new neighborhood until she meets a mysterious Snow Lion, who plays with her and encour-
ages her to meet other children.
Identifiers: LCCN 2017040316 | ISBN 9781682630488
Subjects: | CYAC: Moving, Household—Fiction. | Bashfulness—Fiction. | Friendship—Fiction.
Classification: LCC PZ7.H375916 Sno 2018 | DDC [E]—dc23 LC record available at
*https://lccn.loc.gov/2017040316*

# The
# SNOW LION

## Jim Helmore and Richard Jones

PEACHTREE
ATLANTA

Caro and her mum went to live
in a new house at the top of a hill.

The walls were white, the ceilings were white,
and even the doors were white.

There were lots of places for Caro to explore.
But she wished she had someone to play with.

"How about a game of hide-and-seek?" said a deep, gentle voice.

Caro turned around.

There stood a lion, as white as snow.
"Where did you come from?" Caro asked.

"Oh, here and there,"
said the Snow Lion.

He leaned against the white wall and vanished.
The wall winked at Caro and she laughed.

Caro and the Snow Lion played
hide-and-seek . . .

. . . all day
long.

The next morning, Caro and the Snow Lion looked
out of the window and saw two boys.
Colorful kites swooped and soared.

One of the boys waved, but Caro looked away shyly.

"Come on . . . let's go play," said Caro.

All week, Caro and the Snow Lion
climbed and leaped.

And raced

and chased.

Then, one day, the Snow Lion looked thoughtful.

"Have you tried the slide in the park?" he asked.
"But I like playing here with you," said Caro.

"I'll still be here when you get back,"
the Snow Lion replied.

So Caro went to the park.

When she got there, she found the boy who
had waved at her. The boy's name was Bobby,
and he could play almost as well as the Snow Lion.

"Can't catch me!" Bobby laughed, but by now Caro was very good at chasing.

"How was the slide?" asked the Snow Lion later that night.
"Bumpy!" Caro smiled. "But I missed you."

The next day, Bobby asked Caro if she'd like to play with his friends.

"Give it a try," said the Snow Lion.
"But I won't know anyone," Caro whispered.
"You'll have a great time," said the Snow Lion,
"and you do know Bobby."

So Caro went to Bobby's house,
where they all built a Pirate Spaceship.

After they reached the moon, they buried
their treasure and ate plenty of chocolate cake.

The next morning, Caro's mum said, "I think it's time we put some color in this house, don't you?"

"But I like it white . . . ," said Caro.

Then the doorbell rang.

Her mum had invited all of Caro's new friends for a painting party!

Soon the house was full of oranges, reds, blues, and greens, and by the afternoon everyone needed a bath.

Caro searched everywhere for the Snow Lion that night, but there were no white walls or white ceilings or white doors left.

Outside, it began to snow until the whole hill was covered with white. Down in the garden, something caught Caro's eye.

Could it be?

"I thought I'd never see you again!" cried Caro.

"All lions are happiest outdoors," said the Snow Lion, "and you've got other friends to play with now."

"But I'll miss you."

The Snow Lion smiled. "I'll miss you too. But if you need me, you'll know where to look."

And she did.